A Mad B[...]

A Farce in On[...]

by Isabel McReynolds Gray

BAKER'S PLAYS

Baker's Plays
c/o Samuel French, Inc.
45 West 25 Street
New York, NY 10010
bakersplays.com

A MAD BREAKFAST

CAST OF CHARACTERS

Mrs. Simpkins, *the landlady; of a suspecting disposition and inclined to look on the dark side.*

Lizzie, *the maid-of-all-work; of a melancholy and romantic frame of mind.*

Miss Brown, *young lady boarder, kind-hearted and a general favorite.*

Miss Smith, *another boarder, who, though a stenographer, feels that she would succeed on the stage.*

Miss Green, *also a boarder and an artist, who sees "effects" in unexpected places.*

Mrs. Hill, *a boarder who has "nerves."*

Mr. Hill, *who goes in for spiritualism.*

Mr. Roberts, *a boarder whose appetite is always good.*

Mr. Jones, *a boarder given to practical joking.*

Mr. Long, *who is of an enquiring turn of mind.*

Scene:—The breakfast room of a modest boarding house. Two tables, set for four each. Door from hall. Door to kitchen. Window.

Time:—Six-thirty in the morning—any week day.

Place:—The dining-room in Mrs. Simpkins' boarding house.

Time of Playing:—Forty-five minutes.

A MAD BREAKFAST

(As the curtain rises MRS. SIMPKINS *is discovered laying forks and knives on one table. Enter* LIZZIE *with a tray of cups and saucers.)*

MRS. SIMPKINS. About time to ring the bell, isn't it?

LIZZIE. Not for five minutes yet.

MRS. SIMPKINS. You'd better ring it. They're always late, anyway, and the biscuits is about done.

> [*Exit* MRS. SIMPKINS *to the kitchen.*

*(*LIZZIE *sighs and arranges the cups and takes up a huge bell. Exit* LIZZIE *to the hall, ringing the bell. In the pauses* MR. JONES *laughs. Enter from the hall,* MISS BROWN *and* MR. JONES. *The bell stops.)*

MISS BROWN. (*Looks over the table, sees that breakfast is not served, takes up a newspaper and glances at it.* JONES *continues to read his letter, laughing*) Well, what is so amusing?

JONES. (*Starts to speak, is interrupted by the bell. He continues to laugh. The bell stops*) It's too good to keep. I'll have to share it!

MISS BROWN. What?

JONES. (*Waving the letter*) This!

MISS BROWN. Has someone left you a fortune?

JONES. Read it! (*He gives her the letter.*)

MISS BROWN. (*Taking and reading the letter*) "Mr. Jones: Dear sir: Shall arrive at the institution as soon after six-thirty as possible. Thanking you for providing me with this opportunity for observation and study, I am yours most sincerely, Robert T. Long." (*To* JONES.) What does it mean?

JONES. It's the richest joke since the flood! It means that we're going to have the time of our young lives ——

3

(Bell rings and drowns his voice. He motions wildly and takes a newspaper clipping from his pocket, handing it to MISS BROWN. *The bell stops.)*

MISS BROWN. *(Reading the clipping)* "A middle-aged, well-to-do gentleman of excellent social position would like to visit a small, select private home for the insane, for the purpose of investigation and study. Any information will be gratefully appreciated and well paid for. Address communications to Robert T. Long, Box 2, *Morning Star."*

JONES. Isn't it rich?

MISS BROWN. You don't mean to say——

JONES. I do. I answered his ad. and he answered my answer. *(The bell rings furiously.* JONES *tries to explain to* MISS BROWN *in vain.)* Confound that Lizzie, she'll wake the whole city!

(They gaze at the ad. and the letter until the bell stops.)

MISS BROWN. But where did you send him? His letter says—"shall arrive at the institution as soon after six-thirty as possible——"

JONES. Aha, there's where your Uncle Hennery X. Jones shows what a head he's got!—He's coming here, young lady—he's coming here!

MISS BROWN. What for?

JONES. What for? Suffering cats, the lady asks what for! She has read the ad. and the letter is in her hands. —I would advise a rest cure.

MISS BROWN. I suppose I am dumb, but I don't understand. He wants to see a lunatic asylum, and you invite him here——

JONES. Exactly!

MISS BROWN. But we aren't lunatics!

JONES. Pretty batty bunch, if you ask me.

MISS BROWN. Oh, several of us are a little—queer, I know. But you'll never get him to believe that we're actually insane, you know.

JONES. Not you, dear young lady. I have decided that you shall be my assistant—head nurse of the asylum.

MISS BROWN. And you?

JONES. I am the keeper. (*There is a last furious peal of the bell. Enter* LIZZIE *from the hall. She crosses toward the kitchen door.*) Good-morning, Lizzie!

LIZZIE. (*Mournfully*) Good-morning.

JONES. Have you finished the novel yet?

LIZZIE. No. I'm just on the last chapter. It's awful sad.

MISS BROWN. What is the title of the novel?

LIZZIE. " United in Death." It's awful sad.

MISS BROWN. I'll lend you a good story. It's called "All for Love." It ends happily.

LIZZIE. I like the sad ones best, thank you. They seem more natural.

JONES. You'll be glad to meet the Prince, Lizzie.

(MISS BROWN *gasps. So does* LIZZIE.)

LIZZIE. Huh?

JONES. I don't want it to get around, Lizzie! I don't want a soul but you and Miss Brown to know it.—But Prince James Albert Alfred Edward Henry George, of England, you know, who had such a sad love affair about twenty years ago, when he was just a young boy—— (*Turns to* MISS BROWN.) He fell in love with a pretty girl who waited on the table at the palace, you remember, Miss Brown. She was dismissed, of course, and went to work in a boarding-house. Then the Prince went to live at that boarding-house, incog.! (LIZZIE *gurgles appreciation.*) And when they found that he simply refused to live without this pretty waitress—why, you know—she *disappeared!* Very sad. He spent years searching for her but at last he gave up. Said he knew she was dead or he would have found her. He refused to marry the Princess Patricia Victoria Mary Louise, who broke her heart over him and died in a convent. Now he simply wanders over the world, seeking solace. I can cheer him up, once in a while, but I'm too cheerful to do him any good, really. What he needs is the sympathy of some true womanly heart. It's very sad!

LIZZIE. (*Who has been staring and gurgling with romantic sympathy*) And—he's coming *here?*

JONES. This morning, to breakfast, Lizzie. But he comes simply as Mr. Long. He does not wish to be known. I trust you not to betray him, especially to Mrs. Simpkins, who, I regret to say, is not sympathetic.

LIZZIE. Oh, no, sir! I can keep a secret, I can!

JONES. Remember, he has enemies, Lizzie, who would stoop to any dastardly deed to do him harm!

LIZZIE. (*Shuddering happily*) Trust me, Mr. Jones!
                     [*Exit* LIZZIE *to the kitchen.*

JONES. (*To* MISS BROWN) Do you get the idea?

MISS BROWN. You may deceive poor Lizzie, but the rest won't believe that nonsense.

JONES. Each to his own folly. Everybody here is batty about something—except us, of course! I shall tell our excellent landlady that our inquisitive friend Long is a Secret Service Government Inspector of Boarding Houses, bent on investigating her table.

MISS BROWN. Good heavens! She'll poison him!

(*Enter* MISS SMITH, MR. ROBERTS, MRS. *and* MR. HILL. *General " Good-mornings " and a search for mail at the side table. The* HILLS *take places at the table furthest from the hall door.* ROBERTS *is seated at the other table.* HILL *reads the morning paper and* ROBERTS *gazes morosely at the bare table-cloth in front of him.* MISS BROWN *sits at the table with the* HILLS. LIZZIE *enters with coffee. Enter* MRS. SIMPKINS, *going to the table at which* ROBERTS *is seated.* JONES *detains* MISS SMITH *near the hall door.*)

JONES. Good-morning, Miss Smith!

MISS SMITH. Perhaps it is a good morning, Mr. Jones, but to one of my temperament, mornings is a simply inhuman part of the day. To me day don't begin till one P. M.!

JONES. You should be an actress, Miss Smith.

MISS SMITH. Don't I know it? I'm acting all the time. I've got so much temperament that sometimes the very sight of a typewriter makes me want to scream!

JONES. I wonder you don't leave the office. Go on the stage. I'm sure you've got talent.

MISS SMITH. Mr. Jones, I've got genius—though perhaps you'll think I shouldn't say it about myself—I *know* it! Why, sometimes when I recite "Asleep at the Switch" for the Good Times Club, I make myself cry, my emotions is so real!

JONES. You'd better look out. Some of these managers will snap you up one of these days.

MISS SMITH. Mr. Jones, I never met one.

JONES. You can't say that after to-day.

MISS SMITH. How's that?

JONES. Oh—nothing.—But I may as well tell you in case anything happens. You ought to be prepared in case he does offer you a contract.—Mr. Robert T. Long, Belasco's right-hand man, you know, is coming here to breakfast this morning. Ought to be here now. He goes around like this, you know, looking for new talent. It isn't as easy to find as you might think, Miss Smith. But it's hard to fool Long. He claims he can tell a lot, just from the tone of a girl's voice, about her temperament, and all that.

MISS SMITH. (*Throwing much dramatic fervor into her voice*) Believe me, he can, Mr. Jones! My friends all claim that my voice has the same timbre and a much more sympathetic quality than Ethel Barrymore's!

JONES. I don't know that I've done just the right thing in telling you, Miss Smith. Long is kind of touchy. He likes to do these things on the quiet.

MISS SMITH. You may trust my discretion, Mr. Jones. Introduce him as a bond salesman. I can act a part!

JONES. I'll do that.

(MISS SMITH *takes her place at the table with the* HILLS *and* MISS BROWN, *who enjoys* MISS SMITH'S *dramatic mood.*)

MRS. SIMPKINS. (*Who has been serving breakfast*) Aren't you coming to breakfast, Mr. Jones, or doesn't the food tempt you? I'm sure I do my best, but I'd be glad for any suggestions.

ROBERTS. Might put some coffee in with the chicory. (*He offers his cup for more.*)

MRS. SIMPKINS. (*Filling the cup vindictively*) It's the best I can get, at forty cents a pound. I'm surprised you drink it, Mr. Roberts, if it is so bad.

ROBERTS. Have to drink three cups of this to get one of coffee.

JONES. I—ahem! I'm waiting for someone. May I say a word, Mrs. Simpkins? Pardon me, folks! (*He crosses to* MRS. SIMPKINS, *leans and whispers. She starts as though to leave the table.* JONES *firmly detains her.*) I beg you, do not alarm yourself. You have nothing to fear. I only thought it kinder to prepare you.

MRS. SIMPKINS. I'd better look around a bit.

JONES. Oh, no! Think how badly it would look if he should find you cleaning up, as it were! He might think you had something to hide.

MRS. SIMPKINS. My kitchen's that clean you couldn't soil your pocket handkerchief on it!

JONES. Of course! (*He turns away to hide a smile and observes* MISS [*or* MR.] GREEN *entering.*) Ah, here is Miss Green!

(*Enter from the hall* MISS GREEN, *in painter's smock.* MRS. SIMPKINS *rings for* LIZZIE. *Enter* LIZZIE *from kitchen.*)

MRS. SIMPKINS. (*Aside to* LIZZIE) Throw that hamburger steak in the garbage can!

LIZZIE. But—lunch, mum!

MRS. SIMPKINS. Do as I tell you!

(MISS BROWN, *overhearing, shudders.*)

LIZZIE. Yes, mum!   [*Exit* LIZZIE *to the kitchen.*

JONES. (*Continuing a conversation with* MISS GREEN) You work all the time!

MISS GREEN. I know, but the light was so good! I think this portrait is going to make my fortune—I really do!

MRS. SIMPKINS. (*Elaborately sarcastic*) I suppose old Tony, the peanut man, will buy it to hang in his front parlor!

MISS BROWN. Oh, really, Mrs. Simpkins, we all wish Miss Green success, I'm sure!

MISS GREEN. But Mrs. Simpkins is right. Tony is a good subject, but not a good purchaser. Now, if I could only find a millionaire with an interesting face, who would let me paint it ——

HILL. (*Emerging from the newspaper*) They go to the beauty doctors for that. Haw! (*He gets under cover again.* MISS GREEN *is about to take her place at* MRS. SIMPKINS' *table when* JONES *detains her.*)

JONES. Just a word in confidence, Miss Green. Mr. Robert T. Long is coming here this morning!

MISS GREEN. I don't believe I ever heard of him.

JONES. Never heard of him! Robert T. Long, the multimillionaire? Made his fortune in safety pins?—— He's a queer old fellow. Likes to travel around where he isn't known, and study types.

MISS GREEN. But I don't see ——?

JONES. What this has to do with you? Just a minute. He thinks he has a face like Napoleon—fact! I have it from an intimate friend of his. And old Long gets exceedingly peevish when people can't see the resemblance. Now—if you, as an artist, should discover the resemblance, and tell him ——

MISS GREEN. I see. He might give me an order for a portrait. Thank you! (*Coldly.*) I hope I am not yet reduced to that sort of deception!

JONES. My mistake! Beg pardon. Thought you might like the job.

MRS. SIMPKINS. When may we expect—your *friend,* Mr. Jones?

JONES. Any moment now. I think I'll look out for him. [*Exit* JONES *to the hall.*

MISS GREEN. (*Taking her place at* MRS. SIMPKINS' *table*) Do *you* know Mr. Jones' *friend,* Miss Brown?

MISS BROWN. (*Concealing her amusement*) Oh, yes, I know him, *slightly!*

Miss Green.   They say he is wonderfully like Napoleon!

Miss Brown.   Very!

Miss Smith.   (*Throatily*) They say he can tell all about you, just from the tone of your voice!

Mrs. Simpkins.   All I can say is, he's welcome to come here whenever he pleases. He won't find no skeletons in my closets, though I can't speak for the roomers! (*She removes the molasses jug from* Mr. Roberts' *reach. He is eating industriously, everything in sight. Enter* Lizzie *with food for various boarders. She serves, and listens eagerly to the conversation.*) Have you been getting any messages from the spirit world lately, Mr. Hill?

Mrs. Hill.   (*Wailing*) I should say he has, Mrs. Simpkins! There's been knockings and thumpings and creakings in the wall till I can't get a wink of sleep!

Mr. Hill.   (*Sepulchrally*) There's a warning for someone in this house, though I can't get the message straight!

Mrs. Simpkins.   Maybe it's for me. I had a warning a bit ago.

Miss Smith.   Can warnings be for good news, Mr. Hill?

Mr. Hill.   Good or bad—but mostly bad.

Miss Green.   I take it as a good omen!

Mr. Hill.   Something is in the air! (*He seems to sniff the unseen.*)

Miss Brown.   (*Aside to* Hill) Do you know who is coming? Robert T. Long, the greatest medium that ever lived!

Hill.   Never heard of him!

Miss Brown.   No? Why, he is the reincarnation of Napoleon! Sh!—Everybody—Mr. Long is coming! (*They all rise and face the door.*) Don't appear to notice him! He doesn't like to be noticed! (*They all sit and pretend to eat, listening nervously to voices off.* Miss Brown, *aside to* Lizzie, *whispers.*) Lizzie, don't betray him!

(Lizzie *presses one hand over her mouth, the other to*

her wildly beating heart. ROBERTS, *alone, is eating undisturbed. Enter* JONES *and* LONG.)

JONES. Miss Brown, a word! (MISS BROWN *crosses to the hall door.* MRS. SIMPKINS *and the boarders keep up an elaborate pretense of noting nothing unusual.*) Miss Brown—Mr. Long! (*Aside.*) Mr. Long wishes to see our patients just as they are. Don't disturb them. Let him go among them freely, and mingle. Only, keep an eye on them! That's all!

LONG. (*Nervously*) Is there any danger?

JONES. Not the slightest, as long as you keep an eye on them! Of course, you understand they all have their little ideas. In every case there is some mania, you understand, that must be humored. We never contradict them, always agree with everything they say, but otherwise treat them as if they were quite rational.

LONG. I see! A most humane policy. This is good of you, p-perhaps I have seen enough!

(*As* MRS. SIMPKINS *determinedly takes the molasses jug from* ROBERTS, LONG *thinks he will leave, but is detained by* JONES.)

JONES. By no means! You must mix with them to know them well. (*Raising his voice.*) Ladies and gentlemen, Mr. Robert T. Long!

(*The introduction causes a sensation.*)

MRS. SIMPKINS. (*Rising, placing an extra chair beside herself, and urging* ROBERTS *to move from his place to the new place, making room for* MR. LONG) Sit right down, Mr. Long! This is an *unexpected* pleasure, I'm sure, but you are welcome to anything on the table or in the ice-box!

(*Exit* LIZZIE *precipitately to bring "her Prince" everything in the house.*)

LONG. (*Trembling*) Thank you, I have breakfasted!

MRS. SIMPKINS. (*Aggrieved*) I ain't one to be condemned on hearsay evidence, Mr. Long, that you'll find!

I don't submit to no injustice! Here's the breakfast, as good as I can make it with prices what they is. Take it or leave it, but I'll have justice!

Miss Brown. (*Soothingly*) I'm sure Mr. Long will be charmed to have breakfast with us!

(Roberts *is forced into the new chair, taking his food with him.* Jones *and* Miss Brown *urge* Long *to take the seat vacated, and he does so, unwillingly, under the accusing glare of* Mrs. Simpkins.)

Long. Certainly! Certainly!

(*Enter* Lizzie, *burning with romantic fires, and serves* Long *with hotcakes and coffee.* Long *encounters various glances, fraught with meaning, and shrinks from them.*)

Lizzie. (*Whispering in his ear as she serves him*) My Prince!

Long. EH!

Lizzie. (*Pouring molasses lavishly all over the neighboring table-cloth*) I knowed you! It were my heart as told me!

Long. You know me! (*Pitying one so young and so demented, pats her arm.*) There's a good girl!

(*Exit* Lizzie *to the kitchen, dizzy with bliss.*)

Miss Green. Mr. Long, forgive me! I can't help saying it! I am a painter, you know, and I notice these things more than most. Has anyone ever told you that you look like—*Napoleon?*

Hill. *Look!* He *is* Napoleon! (*To* Long, *who has turned horrified eyes to him.*) As one psychic to another, Mr. Long, don't you sense something *peculiar* in the atmosphere this morning?

Mrs. Simpkins. If you are vulgarly alludin' to the eggs, Mr. Hill, them are the freshest I can get, with prices what they is!

Miss Green. (*Ignoring interruptions and addressing* Mr. Long *with an urgency he cannot resist*) Let me make a portrait of you now as you sit! (MISS GREEN *takes a piece of charcoal from her pocket, maps out a portrait on the table-cloth, squinting and measuring* MR. LONG *as she does so.* MRS. SIMPKINS, *thinking of the laundry bill, protests in vain.* MR. LONG, *afraid to contradict anyone, smiles uneasily, first at* MISS GREEN, *then at* MRS. SIMPKINS. JONES *and* MISS BROWN *are delighted.* HILL, *not to be thwarted, booms.*)

HILL. Mr. Long—as one psychic to another do you, or do you not, sense something in the atmosphere this morning? (LONG *turns to answer* HILL.)

MISS GREEN. (*Frantically sketching, crows hoarsely*) Don't move! Keep the pose!

(LONG *turns back to her without answering* HILL.)

HILL. Do you, or *do you* NOT?

(LONG *turns to him again to answer and is again interrupted by* MISS GREEN.)

MISS GREEN. Perhaps you do not care to have me do you?

LONG. Oh, by all means, go ahead!

MRS. SIMPKINS. By no means, Miss Green! I can't furnish table-cloths for the boarders to draw pictures on, no matter how ambitious they may be to do the portraits of gentlemen as has twenty-five dollars to pay for them!

MISS GREEN. (*Pausing, with her accusing eyes roving from one to another*) Well, I must say ——!

JONES. (*To* MISS GREEN) You must make a portrait of him!

MISS BROWN. Oh, you must! Can't you get a canvas?

HILL. (*With growing excitement*) I'll stake my reputation on it! There's something strange! Some powerful influence is abroad!

MRS. HILL. (*Wailing*) I wish I knew what it was! I'm so nervous!

MISS SMITH. (*Who has been working up a bit of temperament for the benefit of the supposed manager, but who has failed to attract his attention, speaks in a*

*deep " stage voice," breaking in on the reiterated remarks
of all the others*)   My Gawd, what a pandemonium!

(*The force of her remark is such that the others fall
silent for a moment.* MR. ROBERTS *is calmly eating
all this while.* MISS BROWN *and* JONES *are having a
wonderful morning.* MISS GREEN *resumes her
sketching. Enter* LIZZIE *with oatmeal and cream for*
LONG. *She sets them before him and takes a book
from her apron pocket. She studies a line and then
quotes it to him.*)

LIZZIE.   Oh, muh lord, how can one so humble hope
to serve one so ex-al-ted?   (LONG *looks at her in
horror.*)

MISS GREEN.   (*Murmuring as she sketches*)   Napoleon!

MRS. SIMPKINS.   (*Shrilly*)   I can't and I won't have
it, Miss Green!

MISS GREEN.   (*Rising haughtily*)   Very well!   (*To*
LONG, *compellingly.*)   Will you come to my studio, Mr.
Long? It is seldom I get a notion like this, but your face
is *so remarkable!*   (*She continues to " measure" him
with her thumb.* LIZZIE *shows signs of resentment.* MR.
LONG *looks helplessly at* JONES, *who indicates with a nod
and other signs that* LONG *had better humor " the pa-
tient."* LONG *is about to rise and follow* MISS GREEN,
fearfully.)

JONES.   You can't get out of it, I'm afraid, Mr. Long.
You see, Miss Green has the artist's eye.

MRS. SIMPKINS.   (*With determination*)   Not by no
means, Miss Green! Mr. Long is *my* guest and I'll thank
you to let him finish his breakfast!

(LONG *sinks back into his chair, hypnotized by her eye.*
MISS BROWN *signals* LONG *to be careful.*)

MISS BROWN.   Oh, don't disappoint Mrs. Simpkins,
Mr. Long! I won't answer for the consequences if you
do!

MRS. SIMPKINS.   I'm going to give you something of

everything we have, Mr. Long, and I want you should eat it, so you won't be in no doubt regarding *this* boarding house!—That is, if Mr. Roberts has left anything, which I doubt! (*She forcibly takes a plate containing two muffins from* ROBERTS, *who grabs one muffin. The other she bestows upon* LONG. *Exit* LIZZIE *to get more food for her prince.*)

LONG. I'm not hungry, really!

MRS. SIMPKINS. I won't be condemned unheard, Mr. Long, that I won't!

(MISS BROWN, *by signs, advises* LONG *to eat, and the unfortunate tries to do so.*)

HILL. (*To* LONG, *fixing him with a mesmeric eye*) What's your line—cards, palms, or trance?

LONG. I play cards.

HILL. Do you find that spirits help you?

LONG. Yes, indeed! Though I never indulge unless I have a cold. (*He coughs, reaching for his hip pocket.* MRS. SIMPKINS *coughs sympathetically.* HILL *coughs.* MISS SMITH *coughs.* ROBERTS *suspends operations to watch hopefully for whatever will come from* LONG'S *pocket. It proves to be a huge handkerchief, which* LONG *uses to good effect.* HILL *continues the interview.*)

HILL. Do any trance work—materialization?

(*This puzzles* MR. LONG, *who looks to* JONES *for help.*)

JONES. Mr. Hill is a clairvoyant, trance medium, and all that. He can materialize any departed spirit you care to call for!

LONG. Indeed!

MISS BROWN. (*To* LONG) You are a very successful trance medium yourself, aren't you, Mr. Long?

(LONG *is about to deny this, but* MISS BROWN *motions to him to agree.*)

LONG. Oh, yes—rather!

HILL. I thought so! The influence is too strong this

morning! I shouldn't wonder if we could get a materialization right here!

MRS. HILL. Oh, Willyum, not here! Spirits always make me feel so cold!

MRS. SIMPKINS. I'll thank you to let Mr. Long eat his breakfast, Mr. Hill! It sha'n't be said we hid nothing from him!

MISS GREEN. Do hurry, Mr. Long! I want to work while the light is good!   [*Exit* MISS GREEN *to hall.*

MISS SMITH. (*Rising theatrically*) Some people want to hog everything in sight!

(*Enter* LIZZIE *bringing ham and eggs to* LONG. *She speaks aside to him, under cover of serving.*)

LIZZIE. Prince James Albert Alfred Edward George Henery!

LONG. *What!*

LIZZIE. I knowed you—oh, I knowed you!

LONG. Yes, yes, you know me—that's a good girl!

LIZZIE. My heart bleeds for you!

LONG. Never mind, there's a good girl!

MRS. SIMPKINS. Bring more muffins, Lizzie.

LIZZIE. My Prince. (*Exit* LIZZIE, *dizzily, bumping into the door with a crash of dishes.*)

MISS SMITH. (*Feeling that an appropriate time has arrived for a display of temperament*) This place makes me sick! They ain't one of you has a heart! Oh, for a chanst to live! My emotions is too big for this petty grind! I'm in a jail—I'm in a cage!—Somebody break the bars! Oh, great heavens, how I could act, if I had the chanst!

JONES. The chance is bound to come, Miss Smith.

MISS SMITH. (*Who has come down, now whirls about, addressing* LONG) Do *you* think so?

LONG. I?—Oh, yes, indeed!

MISS BROWN. Oh, Miss Smith, do recite "Asleep at the Switch!"

MISS SMITH. I—oh! That's so heavy for the morning, Miss Brown, and I'm not made up! Do you know "Curfew Shall Not Ring To-night"? That's an awful dramatic little thing! (*She delivers two lines in the most exaggerated "elocutionary" manner.*)

"England's sun was slowly setting, o'er the landscape, far away,
Filling all the land with beauty at the close of one sad day."

(*She breaks off abruptly and in contrastingly flat tones speaks to* LONG.) What's your favorite pieces?

LONG. Eh?

JONES. Miss Smith would like to know in which rôles you think she would appear to the greatest advantage. Tragedy?

LONG. (*Desperately taking the cue*) Oh, yes! Shakespeare, by all means!

(MISS SMITH, *almost in a trance herself, moves toward the hall door.*)

MISS SMITH. Give me time to snatch a little make-up, Mr. Long! [*Exit* MISS SMITH *to the hall.*

(LONG *takes out his handkerchief, mops his face, fans himself.* JONES *and* MISS BROWN *exchange wordless congratulations, but* MISS BROWN *is wondering how it will end. Enter* MISS GREEN *with an easel, drawing board and paper, which she sets up. She goes to work at a portrait of* LONG. *When* MRS. SIMPKINS *is not looking,* LONG *puts some of his breakfast in front of* ROBERTS, *who is still busy. Enter* LIZZIE *with more muffins, which are offered to* LONG. LIZZIE *stands smiling and sighing.* MRS. SIMPKINS *discovers* LONG'S *transfer of the food, and resents it.*)

MRS. SIMPKINS. Am I to understand that you are unfriendly disposed, Mr. Long?

LONG. By no means!

JONES. Mr. Long assured me of the greatest interest in you before he came, Mrs. Simpkins.

(*She sniffs. Enter* HILL, *carrying a medium's cabinet*

of black, which he sets up near the hall door. MRS.
HILL *is distressed.*)

MRS. HILL. Oh, Willyum, not spirits!

HILL. We'll just set it up here, Long, and see if we
can't get something! Napoleon, eh?

JONES. Going to materialize a spirit, are you? Fine!
(*Aside to* LONG.) Humor him! He's one of the worst!

LONG. (*Aside to* JONES) I'll just slip away, I believe!

JONES. (*Clutching him*) For heaven's sake, don't!
Let him go on! If you stop him now, I won't take the
consequences!

(LONG *sinks back, overcome with fears.* MISS GREEN
finishes her sketch. HILL *fusses with his cabinet,
and* MRS. HILL *moans.* ROBERTS *continues to eat
and* MRS. SIMPKINS *forcibly takes the butter away
from him.* LIZZIE, *kept near the kitchen door by
her fear of* MRS. SIMPKINS, *darts near enough to*
LONG *once in a while to pull his sleeve or murmur
in his ear.*)

MISS GREEN. (*Showing the sketch*) There! How
do you like it?

JONES. Exactly! That's you, old chap! She's hit
you off! (*Aside to* LONG.) Say something!

LONG. Remarkable! Extraordinary! Wonderful!

MISS GREEN. Do you like it? Shall I finish it?

LONG. Finish a dozen!

MISS GREEN. A dozen!

LONG. Yes, indeed! Send them. (*Aside to* JONES.)
You tell her where to send them.

JONES. (*To* MISS GREEN) I'll attend to that.

MISS GREEN. But you don't understand. I am not a
photographer! You will have to sit for the portrait in
my studio.

LONG. Not this morning, I'm afraid!

HILL. All ready now, old man! We'll pull down the
blinds. (*He does so.*)

MRS. HILL. Oh, Willyum!

(*There is a general movement toward the door.*)

HILL. Everybody sit down, please! Just take hold of hands. I feel sure we'll get something! Concentrate, please!

(*In the darkened room there is still light enough for us to observe that* JONES *has some difficulty in obtaining* ROBERTS' *hand, and finally* JONES *and* MRS. HILL *join hands behind* ROBERTS, *who continues to eat.* LIZZIE *is drawn into the circle and ecstatically grasps the hand of her prince.*)

LIZZIE. Prince Henery, ain't this a sad world?

LONG. Sad, sad, indeed!

MISS GREEN. This makes me nervous! You know, I don't believe in it at all!

HILL. Silence, please! Concentrate! We're *getting it!* (LONG *makes an attempt to leave the table but is restrained by* LIZZIE. *A low, fearsome wail comes from somewhere in the general direction of the cabinet and* LONG *huddles into his chair, to be grasped firmly around the neck by* LIZZIE.) Is someone here?

(*The wail is repeated, louder. All eyes are fixed in superstitious dread upon the cabinet, which is so placed that* MISS SMITH, *made up and draped in a trailing bed spread and bureau scarf, appears to make her entrance from it as she comes from the hall. There are several gasps.*)

MISS SMITH. Romeo, Romeo, where art thou, Romeo? Romeo, Romeo, *Romeo,* ROMEO is muh love, but curfew shall not ring to-night!—Unhand muh, villain! Thy life shalt pay the forfeit!—YOU, Reginald Mortmorency, you came, and with your smiling face, you won muh trusting heart! Curse you! *Curse you!* CURSE YOU!—Romeo, I am going away—away from this place, far, far away, and I have come to say good-bye! All my life I shall love you, Romeo! A rose—a rose! Give me a rose! (*Here she seizes a discouraged stalk of celery which was one of* LIZZIE'S *offerings.*) You, Reginald Mortmorency, curse you! I go—I go—I GO BUT I

SHALL NOT GO ALONE! (*She seizes a table knife and threatens* LONG, *in a tragic pose.*)

(*That gentleman, sliding to the floor, endeavors to get under the table, but* LIZZIE *is still strangling him.* MRS. HILL *has fainted and* JONES *is aiding* MISS BROWN *in attempts to revive her.* HILL *is mad with success.* MISS GREEN, *clutching her sketch, has retreated to a far corner.* ROBERTS *is eating.* MRS. SIMPKINS, *being of a suspicious turn of mind, raises the blind, letting in the morning light.*)

MRS. SIMPKINS.   Spirits indeed! My best bed quilt! (*She snatches at it while the others recover with various emotions.* HILL *is ugly.* MRS. HILL *is relieved.* MISS GREEN *is scornful,* LONG *thankful,* LIZZIE *still clinging.*)

MISS SMITH.   Good dame, lay not thine honest but unlovely hand upon muh gownd!

MRS. SIMPKINS.   Don't you " good dame " me, miss! My hands may be unlovely, though it ain't for you to say so, three weeks behind in your board, and me a-workin' 'em to the bone to keep the place respectable, and you a-trailin' the clean quilt all over the place! (*She snatches the quilt away, leaving* MISS SMITH *in commonplace attire but unaltered mood.*)

MISS SMITH.   (*Sinking down with a moan before* LONG) Deny me not! It is muh life, muh very life! I only want a chanst! Just give me that and all muh life is yours to do with what you will!

(LIZZIE, *recognizing a rival, shows claws.*)

LIZZIE.   Ain't you the brazen piece, Miss Smith? I'd be ashamed! Get away from his hireness! He ain't for such as you!

MISS SMITH.   Worm!

(LIZZIE *hurls herself at* MISS SMITH *and the two clinch in what promises to be a terrific battle, but* LIZZIE *is arrested by* MRS. SIMPKINS *and led firmly to the kitchen door by her ear. She is thrust out.*)

LIZZIE. (*From the kitchen*) Prince! My Prince! (*She makes futile attempts to reënter but is thwarted by* MRS. SIMPKINS.)

HILL. (*Getting his breath at last and inclined to blame* LONG *for the fiasco*) Then—it wasn't a materialization! You faked it!

LONG. No! I assure you!

MISS SMITH. Hear me, where I kneel before you, *you*, YOU! You came, and you brought hope to this poor, suffering heart. You, my IMPRESSARIO!

(*She is answered by a baffled howl from* LIZZIE *beyond the door.*)

MISS GREEN. For pity's sake, Miss Smith, don't monopolize all of the gentleman's time!

HILL. (*Threatening* LONG) If I thought you meant anything——!

JONES. (*Beginning to feel that perhaps this is enough*) Miss Green, if you are to get at that portrait to-day——

MISS GREEN. Yes, I'll go and get things ready at once!

JONES. (*Indicating* LONG) I'll bring him up.

MISS GREEN. Hurry, won't you, Mr. Long? (*She turns at the door.*) So like Napoleon!

[*Exit* MISS GREEN.

JONES. (*Aside to* MISS SMITH, *who is standing in an heroic pose*) That was simply great! You've got him! Now go and get into your best clothes, and we'll all go down to the office and sign a contract!

MISS SMITH. (*Aside to* JONES) Oh, Mr. Jones, is that right? I thought he didn't seem to respond very well!

JONES. You've simply paralyzed him! The man is speechless, but he tipped me the sign. Hurry!

MISS SMITH. I will! (*She crosses to the door, but turns to address* LONG.) Farewell! I shall return anon, and all I wants is a chanst! [*Exit* MISS SMITH.

MRS. SIMPKINS. Mr. Long, you ain't et a thing, and

I don't know as I blame you, the way the boarders has been going on! I'll get you some of my sweet pickle peaches. [*Exit.*

JONES. (*Aside to* LONG) You'd better get away now, I think! You've seen them at their best.

LONG. (*Gratefully*) Yes, yes! I'll go! It has all been very interesting!

HILL. (*Taking up his cabinet, speaking to* LONG) If I thought you meant anything!

JONES. Mr. Hill, Mr. Long is one of Europe's most famous mediums. Do you think he'd have anything to do with that little two-cylinder affair?

HILL. I'll have you understand that I've materialized before the crowned heads of Europe!

JONES. Well, Mr. Long, what do you say? Will you come over some evening? (*Aside.*) Better agree!

LONG. Yes! Oh, yes, any other time!

MRS. HILL. Oh, Willyum, not in the evening!

HILL. Well—I'll give you one more chance!

[*Exeunt* MRS. *and* MR. HILL, *haughtily.*

JONES. (*Urging* LONG *toward the hall door*) Now here is your chance to make a getaway before any of them come back!

LONG. My dear sir, I thank you! (*Taking out his pocketbook.*) My dear sir, the experience has been immensely valuable! My paper will be read before the Eutopia Club. I fancy it will create a sensation! I have only two hundred and fifty-odd dollars, but I will write a check for a thousand if you say the word!

JONES. No! No, thank you! (*With great strength of mind he puts aside the money offered by* LONG *and exchanges sad glances with* MISS BROWN.)

LONG. (*Still offering the bills*) Not for yourself, I understand! But for the institution. Some little entertainment for the unfortunates, perhaps, or (*glancing at the table*) some trifling delicacies! (JONES *and* MISS BROWN *decline to take the money.*) The experience has been worth more than this! And to think that I am getting out of it safe and sound! Thanks to you and Miss Brown!

JONES. Oh, there wasn't the slightest danger—as long as we had our eye on them!

MISS BROWN. Wouldn't it be best for Mr. Long to go now? Some of them may return at any moment!

LONG. By all means! (*Again offering the bills to* JONES.) Do take this!

JONES. Couldn't take it, really!

MISS BROWN. It would be false pretenses, you know.

LONG. (*Growing suspicious*) Eh? (*He puts the money on the table.*)

JONES. I owe you an apology, Mr. Long. Those people are not insane.

LONG. *Not insane?*

JONES. No more insane than I am.

LONG. Not any more insane than you are?—Oh, I see! (*He edges away from* JONES.)

MISS BROWN. He is perfectly right, Mr. Long. Please take your money. We might be arrested!

LONG. (*Extremely nervous, backing toward the door, keeping his eye on them*) I'll be going, I think!

JONES. (*To* MISS BROWN, *pointing to the bills*) You make him take it. We can't keep it.

MISS BROWN. (*Taking the money and trying to press it into* LONG's *hand*) Take it, please! I insist!

JONES. (*Aside to* MISS BROWN) Here comes someone! Get him out!

MISS BROWN. Come, come! (*Aside to* LONG, *pointing to* JONES.) He may become dangerous! Do go! (*She succeeds in forcing the bills into* LONG's *hand.*)

JONES. (*Aside to* LONG, *pointing to* MISS BROWN) I won't answer for the consequences if you enrage her!

LONG. Good heavens, both of them mad!

(*Enter* LIZZIE *in her terrible best, carrying her bag. She has been fired or has quit.*)

LIZZIE. My Prince!

LONG. (*Putting the money into* LIZZIE's *outstretched hand*) Here! Take this—to remember me by!

[*Exit* LONG, *hastily.*

JONES. (*Staring at the money*)   Two hundred and fifty!

LIZZIE.   Prince, oh, Prince Alfred Albert George —— (*She rushes after* LONG.   *Exit.*)

(JONES *and* MISS BROWN *collapse.*   MR. ROBERTS *reaches over for the chocolate cake and continues his breakfast.*)

CURTAIN

OTHER TITLES AVAILABLE FROM BAKER'S PLAYS

HOW THE OTHER HALF LOVES

Alan Ayckbourn

Farce / 3m, 3f / interior

There are three couples in this play; the men all work for the same firm. One of the younger men is having an affair with the wife of the oldest. When each returns home suspiciously late one night, they invent a story about having to smooth domestic troubles for the third couple.

OTHER TITLES AVAILABLE FROM BAKER'S PLAYS

KISS ME QUICK, I'M DOUBLE PARKED

John Kirkpatrick

Farce / 5m, 7f / interior

Things were hectic in the office of Alex, a young dentist. On his way to get married, his bride was marooned on the twenty-second floor by an elevator strike, and his secretary was not sympathetic. When the garbage collectors tried to cross the picket lines, there were demonstrations by the parents and teachers from the public school on the corner. When you add to this the Con Edison people digging up the sidewalk, a masked bandit and a broken gas main which threatens to blow up the building, is it any wonder that Alex almost eloped with the wrong woman?

OTHER TITLES AVAILABLE FROM BAKER'S PLAYS

EVERYBODY'S CRAZY

Jay Tobias

Farce / 8m, 7f / interior

Three young college men take on more than they can handle when they buy a summer hotel. Business is bad — so very bad that it becomes necessary to give the hotel a reputation as a haven for ghosts, and the secret hiding place of an old miser's hoard of gold. That brings in the guests — though perhaps not the kind the young men are looking for: an elderly spiritualist, a sleep-walking Romeo and his hypochondriac wife, and a farmer prone to nightmares. One of the boys impersonates a doctor and treats the guests for all sorts of imagined ailments, another assumes a feminine disguise and sets many a masculine heart beating!